WINTER

WINTER
A Solstice Story

Kelsey E. Gross   Renata Liwska

A Paula Wiseman Book
Simon & Schuster Books for Young Readers
NEW YORK LONDON TORONTO SYDNEY NEW DELHI

Owl watches as

sunlight dims to a shimmer
and starlight scatters across snow dust.
Tonight is the longest night of the year.

Solstice is here.

Owl swoops down
and calls from his perch in the frosted pine,

Whooo can help me shine the light,
and share a gift of hope this night?

Deer nestles nuts on branches,
gifts of hope
that all creatures have enough to eat.

I can help to shine the light!

Squirrel rests leaves on limbs,
gifts of hope
for shelter when it storms.

I can help to share the light!

Mouse sprinkles seeds,
gifts of hope
for blossoming growth.

I can help to spread the light!

Duck tucks feathers amongst the boughs,
gifts of hope
for warm, cozy beds.

I can help to show the light!

Rabbit tosses bits of bark,
gifts of hope
for happy celebrations.

I can help send out the light!

Raccoon stows berries in the snow,
gifts of hope
for sweet surprises.

I can help to spark the light!

Chickadee wraps grasses round and round,
gifts of hope
for loving hugs.

I can help to shine the light!

Owl nods and unfolds his wings.

Love's light will flow beyond our tree,
across the land, the sky, and sea.
The stars glow bright this time of year.

Bounding, twirling, soaring, hopping,
they frolic and sing
around the tree.

Until . . .

Footsteps thump.

Twigs snap.

All the animals freeze.

Owl welcomes the new friend.

Let every creature see our tree!
Its splendor is a gift of light
and hope for all
this winter's night.

For Simon, my shining light
—K. G.

To memories of the past and promises of the future
—R. L.

SIMON & SCHUSTER BOOKS FOR YOUNG READERS
An imprint of Simon & Schuster Children's Publishing Division
1230 Avenue of the Americas, New York, New York 10020
Text © 2023 by Kelsey E. Gross
Illustration © 2023 by Renata Liwska
Book design by Chloë Foglia © 2023 by Simon & Schuster, Inc.

SIMON & SCHUSTER BOOKS FOR YOUNG READERS
and related marks are trademarks of Simon & Schuster, Inc.
For information about special discounts for bulk purchases, please contact Simon & Schuster
Special Sales at 1-866-506-1949 or business@simonandschuster.com.
The Simon & Schuster Speakers Bureau can bring authors to your live event. For more
information or to book an event, contact the Simon & Schuster Speakers
Bureau at 1-866-248-3049 or visit our
website at www.simonspeakers.com.
The text for this book was set in English Engravers.
The illustrations for this book were rendered digitally.
Manufactured in China
0623 SCP
First Edition
2 4 6 8 10 9 7 5 3 1
Library of Congress Cataloging-in-Publication Data
Names: Gross, Kelsey Ebben, 1982– author. | Liwska, Renata, illustrator.
Title: Winter : a solstice story / Kelsey E. Gross ; illustrated by Renata Liwska.
Description: First edition. | New York : Simon & Schuster Books for Young Readers, [2023] | "A Paula
Wiseman Book." | Audience: Ages 4–8. | Audience: Grades 2–3. | Summary: Owl and his friends gather up
gifts of hope from the woodlands to help shine the light on the longest night of the year.
Identifiers: LCCN 2022046636 (print) | LCCN 2022046637 (ebook) |
ISBN 9781665908139 (hardcover) | ISBN 9781665908146 (ebook)
Subjects: CYAC: Winter solstice—Fiction. | Forest animals—Fiction. | LCGFT: Animal fiction. | Picture books.
Classification: LCC PZ7.1.G783 Wi 2023 (print) | LCC PZ7.1.G783 (ebook) | DDC [E]—dc23
LC record available at https://lccn.loc.gov/2022046636
LC ebook record available at https://lccn.loc.gov/2022046637